WAKE UP, CITY!

For Dorothy Briley—with many thanks!

Text copyright © 1957, 1990 by Alvin Tresselt
Illustrations copyright © 1990 by Carolyn Ewing
Inquiries should be addressed to Lothrop, Lee & Shepard Books, a division of William
Morrow & Company, Inc., 105 Madison Avenue, New York, New York 10016. Printed in the
United States of America.

First Edition 1 2 3 4 5 6 7 8 9 10

Library of Congress Cataloging in Publication Data
Tresselt, Alvin R. Wake up, city! / by Alvin Tresselt; illustrated by Carolyn Ewing.   p.
cm. Summary: Describes all the many things that begin to happen as morning comes to the
city. ISBN 0-688-08652-7.—ISBN 0-688-08653-5 (lib. bdg.) [1. Day—Fiction.
2. City and town life—Fiction.]   I. Ewing, C. S. ill.   II. Title. PZ7.T732Wak
1990   [E]—dc20
89-45901 CIP AC

ALVIN TRESSELT

WAKE UP, CITY!

PICTURES BY CAROLYN EWING

LOTHROP, LEE & SHEPARD BOOKS   NEW YORK

Under the stars the city sleeps.
Only the police officers are about, walking their beat.
Only an alley cat, prowling a backyard fence.
Only a mother, rocking her baby back to sleep.

Then slowly the eastern sky begins to brighten.
Here a light goes on…there a light goes on,
as people stir and waken.

The city sparrows begin to cheep.
And the ducks on the pond in the park
call to one another across the black water.

The city is waking in the dim dawn light,
and the tops of tall buildings glow
in the first rays of the rising sun.
The police officers sniff the fresh morning air.
"It looks like another great day!" they say to each other.

In the garages buses are ready for the day's work.
The gas tanks are full and the windshields are clean.
The bus drivers straighten their caps and hop aboard,
and off go the big buses, rolling down the street.

In the harbor a great freighter from across the world
comes in on the morning tide.
Tugboats and harbor patrols
are all ready for a busy day.

At the docks fishing boats unload tubs
of fresh-caught fish from the sea.
Salmon and tuna, claw-wiggling crabs and lobsters,
and hard-shelled clams and oysters.

Down in the noisy markets workers are unloading trucks
filled with refrigerated food.
Crates of lettuce, bags of onions, boxes of oranges.
Fresh fruits and vegetables for the city
from faraway farms.

As the police officers walk back to the station house, they hear the *brrrring* of alarm clocks.
A radio voice tells them today will be fair and cooler, and they hear the babies crying for their breakfast.

With a clank and a crunch and a rumble
the garbage trucks grind through the streets.
A sprinkler truck leaves a trail of shiny wet pavement
to catch the dawn-pink sky overhead.

The corner store is open, with stacks of crisp newspapers piled up in front.
Fair and cooler, says the weather report,
with moderate winds.
Barometer steady.
From open windows comes the smell of perking coffee and sizzling bacon,

the pop of toasters, and the voices of mothers calling,
"Hurry up, you'll be late!"
Now the streets hum with the hustle and bustle and jostle
of the traffic.

With a honk and a toot and a start and a stop
the trucks and buses and taxis crowd
through the busy streets.
And jets zoom overhead, coming in for a landing,
with passengers from everywhere.

Workers hurry to their jobs in the tall office buildings.
People at home are busy making beds
and washing up the breakfast dishes.
And children are in school, ready for a new day.
GOOD MORNING!

Alvin Tresselt writes for very young children in a very special way. Using the simplest, clearest language, he introduces readers to the basic facts and moods of the world around them. Noted for the poetic quality of the author's prose, his books have awakened thousands of readers and listeners to the many small miracles of life. *Rain Drop Splash*, with illustrations by Leonard Weisgard, was a Caldecott Honor Book in 1946, and *White Snow, Bright Snow*, illustrated by Roger Duvoisin, was the winner of the 1947 Caldecott Medal.

Wake Up, City! was first published in 1957 with illustrations by Roger Duvoisin. Mr. Tresselt has updated the text of this new edition, enhancing its appeal to a modern generation of children. New full-color paintings by Carolyn Ewing provide a fresh, contemporary setting.

Mr. Tresselt lives in Redding, Connecticut. Ms. Ewing lives in Kansas City, Missouri.